JoJo & Gran Gran

This JoJo & Gran Gran story book belongs to:

____

First published in Great Britain in 2021 by Pat-a-Cake
Pat-a-Cake is a registered trademark of Hodder & Stoughton Limited

Based on original characters by Laura Henry-Allain
Additional images © Shutterstock
ISBN 978 1 52638 337 2
3 5 7 9 10 8 6 4
Pat-a-Cake, an imprint of Hachette Children's Group,
Part of Hodder & Stoughton Limited
Carmelite House, 50 Victoria Embankment, London EC4Y 0DZ
An Hachette UK Company
www.hachette.co.uk - www.hachettechildrens.co.uk
Printed and bound in Spain
A CIP catalogue record for this book is available from the British Library

JoJo & GranGran

GO TO THE BEACH

Picture Glossary

Here are some words from JoJo's visit to the beach.

JoJo

Gran Gran

Monty

bus

beach

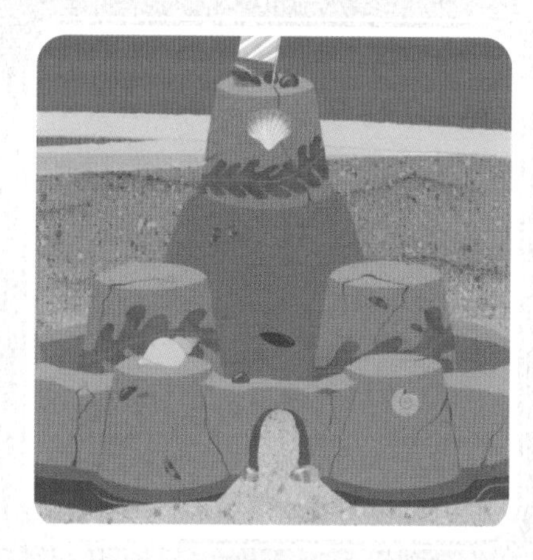

sandcastle

bucket

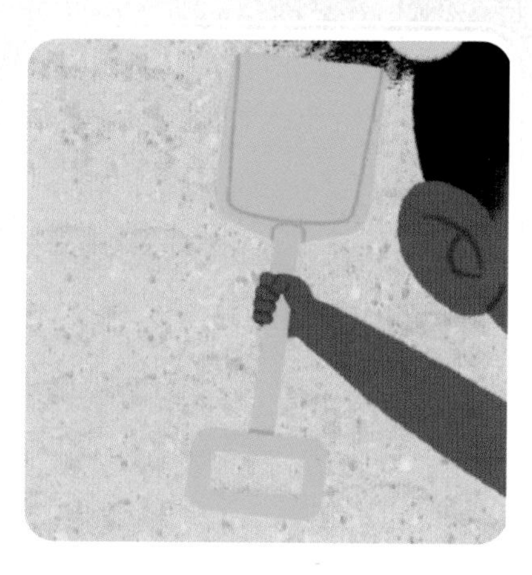

spade

shell

ice cream

It was a summer day, the sky was blue, and JoJo and Gran Gran were going on a trip to the beach. JoJo was very excited.

"Panda can't wait to build a sandcastle, can you, Panda?" giggled JoJo.

On the bus, JoJo looked out of the window, jiggled up and down, swung her legs and then asked . . .

“Are we there, Gran Gran?”

“Soon,” Gran Gran replied.

JoJo looked out of the window again, she jiggled up and down, she swung her legs and then she asked . . .

"How about now?"

Gran Gran smiled.

"We're on a bus, JoJo, not a speedy rocket!"

"Weeee!" said JoJo, whizzing Panda through the air like a rocket.

JoJo and Gran Gran looked out of the window one more time.

"Ah!" said Gran Gran. "We're getting close. Can you see, JoJo?"

JoJo looked hard.

"The beach!" she squealed in delight.

JoJo and Gran Gran got off the bus and headed to the beach.

Gran Gran's friend Ned and his dog Monty got off the bus, too.

“Nice day for the beach,” said Ned.

“We are going to build a sandcastle!” shouted JoJo.

JoJo ran down the beach and cartwheeled her way towards the sea.

“Weee!” she whooped as she turned cartwheel after cartwheel.

JoJo found a space on the beach, and Gran Gran planted the big parasol into the sand.

"Aah, this is the perfect spot, JoJo," she said. "The tide is still quite far out so there's plenty of room to build our sandcastle. Time to get to work!"

“Bucket?” said Gran Gran.

JoJo held up her red bucket. “Bucket!” she yelled.

“Spade?” said Gran Gran.

JoJo held up her green spade. “Spade!” she cried.

“Let’s get building!”

They both filled their buckets with wet sand. Gran Gran turned her bucket over first. She tapped it with her spade and lifted it up. Then, JoJo turned her bucket over on top of Gran Gran's, making a tower. "This can be your sandcastle, Panda," said JoJo.

Suddenly, there was a cry. "Look out!"
JoJo looked up and there was a big beach ball heading straight for the sandcastle . . . and Panda!
She grabbed Panda just in time.

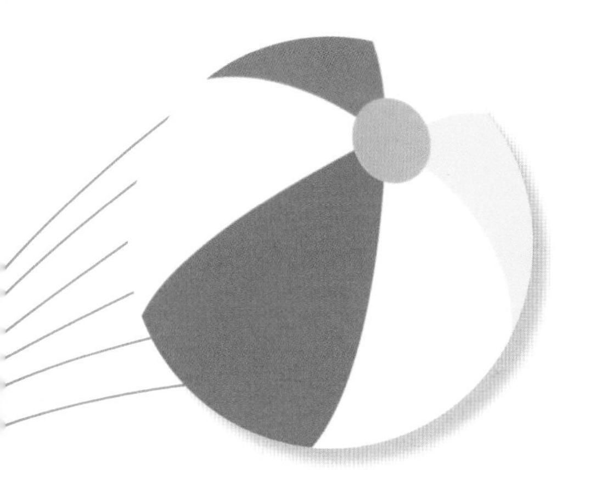

The beach ball crashed into the sandcastle. All that was left was a hole in the sand.
"Oh no . . ." said JoJo, sadly.
"It's OK, JoJo, we can build another sandcastle. And this one will be even bigger and better!" said Gran Gran.

JoJo and Gran Gran started to build a new sandcastle, even better than the first one. JoJo was too excited to notice that the waves seemed to be a little closer to them than when they arrived.

Soon, they were decorating the sandcastle with some shells and seaweed.

"Nothing will knock this one down, Panda," she said as she put him in the middle of the castle.

Just then, Monty ran over to them.

"Hello, Monty, do you like our sandcastle?" asked JoJo.

"Monty!" called Ned.

As Monty raced back towards Ned, he ran straight through the sandcastle, knocking it over.

"Our biggest, best sandcastle ever is all ruined . . . again!" said JoJo.

"Sorry!" shouted Ned.

“OK, Panda,” said JoJo, picking up her spade again. “You will get your sandcastle. And this time, it will be the biggest, best, most amazing sandcastle ever!”

And with that, JoJo and Gran Gran started to build the new sandcastle.

"Ta-dah!" cried JoJo and Gran Gran.

"The biggest, best, most amazing sandcastle ever!" shouted JoJo.

"Do you know what builders of the biggest, best, most amazing sandcastle need to do next?" asked Gran Gran, laughing.

“Build more sandcastles?” JoJo replied.

“Have an ice cream!” said Gran Gran.

“And then, we build more sandcastles?” asked JoJo.

“Not today, JoJo. The tide’s coming in,” replied Gran Gran.

“What’s the tide?” JoJo said.

"It's how the sea comes in and out – when it's low tide the waves are much further away but when it's high tide the waves cover the whole beach."

"The whole beach?"

"Yes, the waves will wash away the sandcastle. So, when the tide goes back out again, the beach will look brand new."

JoJo looked sad as she picked up Panda.

“Sorry, Panda,” whispered JoJo as she cuddled him. “The tide is coming in so the waves will wash our sandcastle away soon.”

Looking at JoJo and Panda, Gran Gran had an idea to make things better. “Hmm . . . I think it’s time for a Gran Gran plan,” she said, taking her tablet out of her bag.

“We can take some pictures of Panda and the sandcastle. So, even when the tide’s washed it away, we can remember what the best sandcastle ever looked like!”

“Yay!” JoJo cheered, posing Panda for his photos.

Once JoJo had pictures of Panda and the sandcastle, she felt much better.

Now it was definitely time for ice cream.

JoJo and Gran Gran ate their ice creams on a bench overlooking the beach.

“Can we make the tide stop coming in?” asked JoJo.

“No, the tide always comes in and always goes out again.
We can’t change that. But we can always build another sandcastle another day,” said Gran Gran.

"Goodbye, sandcastle," said JoJo

as the sea gently . . .

washed it all away.

Once JoJo and Gran Gran were back at home, they looked at all the lovely photos from the beach.

"Now we will always remember our fun day at the beach," said Gran Gran. "And the biggest, best, most amazing sandcastle ever!"

"I love you, Gran Gran," said JoJo as she snuggled up.

"Ahh, I love you too, JoJo!" replied Gran Gran.

Sort the Sandcastles

JoJo and Gran Gran had lots of fun building sandcastles at the beach.
Can you put these sandcastles in order from smallest to biggest?
Use your finger to point at each one in order.